For every clever little monkey!

Based on original illustrations by Jo Ryan

This book was made by Mara van der Meer,
Penny Worms, and Kate Ward.

Copyright © 2017 St. Martin's Press
175 Fifth Avenue, New York, NY 10010

Created for St. Martin's Press by priddy books

1 3 5 7 9 10 8 6 4 2

Manufactured in China January 2017

Charlie
the
Champ

Roger Priddy & Stephen Woods
Illustrated by Lindsey Sagar

I'm the fastest.

To the east of the Limpopo,
by some cool freshwater springs,
the animals were arguing
over who was best at things.

Let's have a competition then, a sort of Jungle Games.

"Good idea!" they all agreed.
"A chance to prove our claims!"

But Charlie Chimp, she felt so sad.
She'd never won a prize.
She wished there was a competition
just for being wise.

Just do your best, Charlie.

The games began with racing
down the narrow, dusty track.
The whistle blew and off they ran,
leaving Charlie at the back!

But looking up, she saw her chance,
as Lion won the race.
She grabbed a vine and flew
right through the air to second place!

"First to cross the river"
was the next trial of the day.
But little Charlie worried
that she might get swept away.

The whistle blew and Crocodile sped off—
he couldn't fail!
But clever Charlie grabbed a ride
by clinging to his tail!

Hide-and-Seek was next—
to find a place that they could squeeze.
Poor Hippo had a problem
trying to hide behind the trees!

Charlie thought she'd won this time.
She curled up in a ball.

But Chameleon turned the color of a tree
and fooled them all.

For the final test, the Tug-of-War,
Team Rhino took the strain.
The others huffed and puffed,
but it was hopelessly in vain.

So little Charlie, thinking fast,
just pulled a funny face.

She made them laugh, and put them off.
Team Charlie got first place!

And later, at a party
lit with stars and fireflies,
they cheered as little Charlie
won the "Cheeky Monkey" prize!